This book is for all the children who dare to dream. My dreamers
are Melanie, Jillian, Devin, and Sasha. Special thanks to my Dad,
who read to me every night and always believed in my dreams.
—V.W.

To my parents, Saralyn and Tim
—T.N.W

STERLING CHILDREN'S BOOKS
New York

An Imprint of Sterling Publishing Co., Inc.
1166 Avenue of the Americas
New York, NY 10036

Based on the song written by Rick Knowles.

ISBN 978-1-4549-3834-7

Distributed in Canada by Sterling Publishing Co., Inc.
c/o Canadian Manda Group, 664 Annette Street
Toronto, Ontario M6S 2C8, Canada
Distributed in the United Kingdom by GMC Distribution Services
Castle Place, 166 High Street, Lewes, East Sussex BN7 1XU, England
Distributed in Australia by NewSouth Books, University of New South Wales, Sydney, NSW 2052 Australia

For information about custom editions, special sales, and premium and corporate purchases,
please contact Sterling Special Sales at 800-805-5489 or specialsales@sterlingpublishing.com.

Manufactured in China
Lot #:
2 4 6 8 10 9 7 5 3 1
02/20

sterlingpublishing.com

Cover and interior design by Heather Kelly

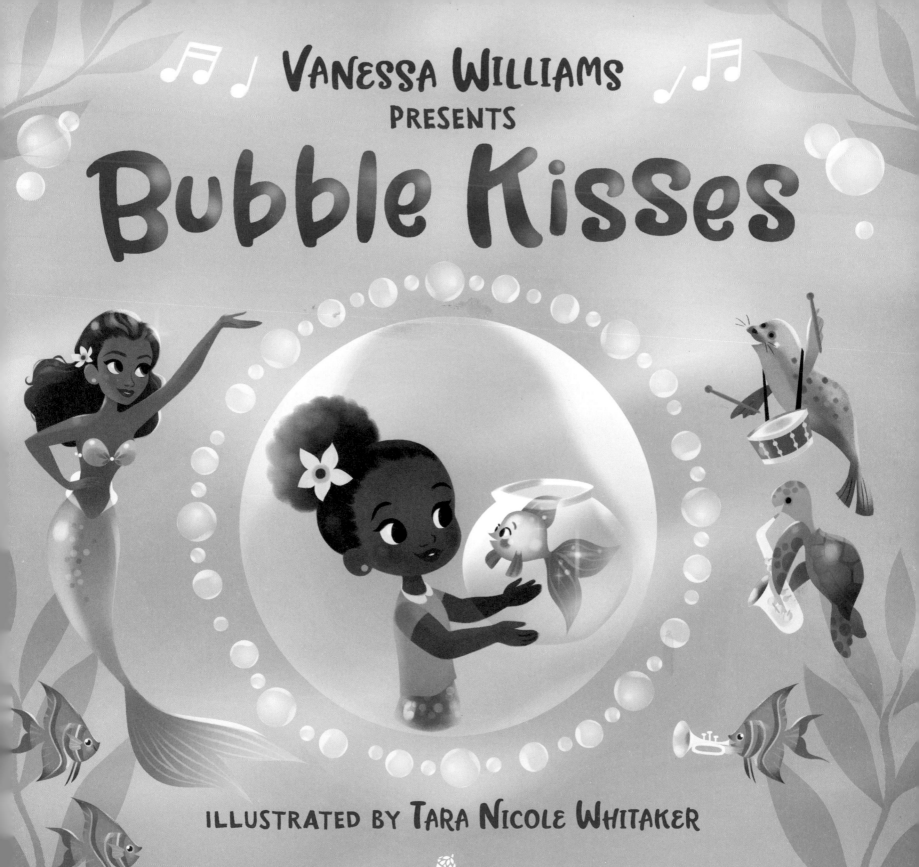

VANESSA WILLIAMS

PRESENTS

Bubble Kisses

ILLUSTRATED BY TARA NICOLE WHITAKER

STERLING CHILDREN'S BOOKS
New York

I got a goldfish,
and her name is Sal.

She's not just a pet.
She's my pal.

We play lots of games together
though they're all pretend.
And the other kids wonder why
she's such a special friend.

She can't roar like a lion,
bark like a dog,

scratch like a cat,
or jump like a frog.

run like a deer,
or do a hummingbird hover.

But here's the reason that I really love her.

She gives me bubble kisses, bubble kisses
as she swims by in the water.

She never misses with her bubble kisses.
And I'm so glad I got her.

Bubble kisses, so delicious,
are usually just for other fishes.

From people's lives such things are missing
as bub-bub-bub-bub-bubble kisses.

Bubble kisses, so delicious,
are usually just for other fishes.

From people's lives such things are missing
as bub-bub-bub-bub-bubble kisses.

She can't roar like a lion,
bark like a dog.

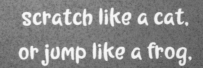

scratch like a cat,
or jump like a frog.

Though she can't do a lot of things this is true,
I'm glad for the one thing she can really do.

She gives me bubble kisses, bubble kisses
as she swims by in the water.
She never misses with her bubble kisses.
And I'm so glad I got her.

Bubble kisses, so delicious,
are usually just for other fishes.

From people's lives such things are missing
as bub-bub-bub-bub-bubble kisses.

Bubble kisses, bubble kisses
as she swims by in the water.

Bubble kisses, so delicious,
are usually just for other fishes.

From people's lives such things are missing
as bub-bub-bub-bub-bubble kisses.

With the funny, lovely Sal.